P9-DCN-741

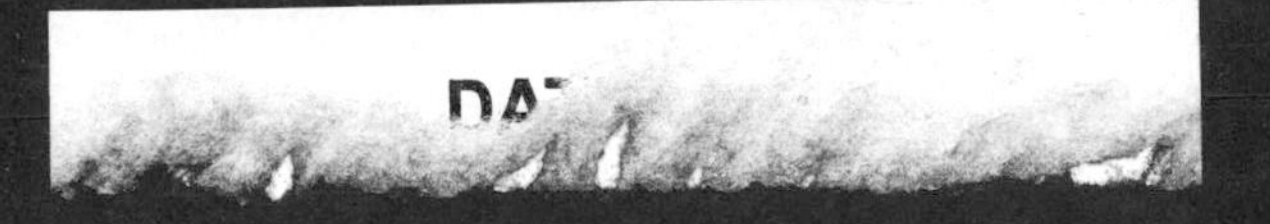
DAT

A Note to Parents and Teachers

Kids can imagine, kids can laugh and kids can learn to read with this exciting new series of first readers. Each book in the Kids Can Read series has been especially written, illustrated and designed for beginning readers. Humorous, easy-to-read stories, appealing characters, and engaging illustrations make for books that kids will want to read over and over again.

To make selecting a book easy for kids, parents and teachers, the Kids Can Read series offers three levels based on different reading abilities:

Level 1: Kids Can Start to Read

Short stories, simple sentences, easy vocabulary, lots of repetition and visual clues for kids just beginning to read.

Level 2: Kids Can Read with Help

Longer stories, varied sentences, increased vocabulary, some repetition and visual clues for kids who have some reading skills, but may need a little help.

Level 3: Kids Can Read Alone

Longer, more complex stories and sentences, more challenging vocabulary, language play, minimal repetition and visual clues for kids who are reading by themselves.

With the Kids Can Read series, kids can enter a new and exciting world of reading!

Sam Finds a Monster

Written by Mary Labatt

Illustrated by Marisol Sarrazin

Kids Can Press

Kids Can Press acknowledges the financial support of the Ontario Arts Council, the Canada Council for the Arts and the Government of Canada, through the BPIDP, for our publishing activity.

Published in Canada by
Kids Can Press Ltd.
29 Birch Avenue
Toronto, ON M4V 1E2

Published in the U.S. by
Kids Can Press Ltd.
2250 Military Road
Tonawanda, NY 14150

www.kidscanpress.com

Edited by David MacDonald
Designed by Stacie Bowes and Marie Bartholomew
Printed and bound in China

The hardcover edition of this book is smyth sewn casebound.
The paperback edition of this book is limp sewn with a drawn-on cover.

CM 03 0 9 8 7 6 5 4 3 2
CM PA 03 0 9 8 7 6 5 4 3 2

National Library of Canada Cataloguing in Publication Data

Labatt, Mary, 1944–
Sam finds a monster / written by Mary Labatt ; illustrated by Marisol Sarrazin.

(Kids can read)

ISBN-13: 978-1-55337-351-3 (bound).
ISBN-10: 1-55337-351-0 (bound).

ISBN-13: 978-1-55337-352-0 (pbk.)
ISBN-10: 1-55337-352-9 (pbk.)

I. Sarrazin, Marisol, 1965– II.Title. III. Series: Kids can read (Toronto, Ont.)

PS8573.A135S24 2003 jC813'.54 C2002-901432-8PZ7

Kids Can Press is a Corus™ Entertainment company

Sam was watching TV.

She saw a big green monster.

It was a scary monster.

The big green monster

scared everybody.

Then it ran away.

Sam sat up.

She stared at the TV.

The big green monster was gone!

"Where did the monster go?"

thought Sam.

"Maybe it came here!

I will find that big green monster."

"Where do monsters hide?"

thought Sam.

"Monsters hide under beds."

She looked under the bed.

"No big green monster here."

"Monsters hide behind sofas,"

thought Sam.

She looked behind the sofa.

"No big green monster here."

“Monsters hide under tables,”

thought Sam.

She looked under the table.

“No big green monster here.”

"Monsters hide in kitchens,"

thought Sam.

She looked in the kitchen.

"No big green monster here."

Then Sam saw the closet door.

It was open.

It was dark in the closet.

"Gr-r-r-r," said Sam.

Sam peeked in the closet.

"Yikes!" thought Sam.

"It's the big green monster!"

The big green monster

looked at Sam.

Sam looked at

the big green monster.

“Gr-r-r-r,” said Sam. “Woof!”

But the big green monster didn’t move.

Sam jumped up and down.

"Woof!" said Sam.

"Woof! Woof!"

But the big green monster didn't move.

Sam showed her teeth.

But the big green monster didn't move.

"Hmmm," thought Sam.

"I can make that monster move."

Sam bit the monster's foot

and pulled.

This time the monster moved!

"Gr-r-r-r," said Sam.

A bit of the big green monster came off!

Something fell out!

Sam sniffed.

"I smell cookies!" she thought.

"Hmmm," thought Sam.

"I know why

this big green monster came.

This monster came to eat my cookies!"

Sam glared at the monster.

"No more cookies for you, Monster!"

thought Sam.

Sam bit the monster's other foot
and pulled.

"Gr-r-r-r," said Sam.

Another bit of the big green monster

came off!

Something fell out!

Sam sniffed.

"I smell donuts!" she thought.

"Hmmm," thought Sam.

"I know why

this big green monster came.

This monster came to eat my donuts!"

Sam glared at the monster.

"No more donuts for you, Monster!"

thought Sam.

Sam shook the monster.

"Gr-r-r-r," said Sam.

Bones and cake and pizza bits

flew around the kitchen.

Sam stopped

and looked around.

“Hmmm,” thought Sam.

“Where did that big green monster go?”

Sam looked under the table.

She looked behind the sofa

and under the bed.

The big green monster was gone.

The door opened and

Joan and Bob came in.

Sam ran to the door.

"Oh, no!" said Joan.

"What a mess!" said Bob.

"Who cares about the mess?"

thought Sam.

"I'm a hero!"

"I chased the big green monster away!"